Lull-a-bye, Little One

Dianne Ochiltree ✱ Illustrated by Hideko Takahashi

G. P. Putnam's Sons

G. P. PUTNAM'S SONS
A division of Penguin Young Readers Group.
Published by The Penguin Group.
Penguin Group (USA) Inc., 375 Hudson Street, New York, NY 10014, U.S.A.
Penguin Group (Canada), 90 Eglinton Avenue East, Suite 700, Toronto, Ontario, Canada M4P 2Y3
(a division of Pearson Penguin Canada Inc.).
Penguin Books Ltd, 80 Strand, London WC2R 0RL, England.
Penguin Ireland, 25 St. Stephen's Green, Dublin 2, Ireland (a division of Penguin Books Ltd.).
Penguin Group (Australia), 250 Camberwell Road, Camberwell, Victoria 3124, Australia
(a division of Pearson Australia Group Pty Ltd).
Penguin Books India Pvt Ltd, 11 Community Centre, Panchsheel Park, New Delhi - 110 017, India.
Penguin Group (NZ), Cnr Airborne and Rosedale Roads, Albany, Auckland 1310, New Zealand
(a division of Pearson New Zealand Ltd).
Penguin Books (South Africa) (Pty) Ltd, 24 Sturdee Avenue, Rosebank, Johannesburg 2196, South Africa.
Penguin Books Ltd, Registered Offices: 80 Strand, London WC2R 0RL, England.

Library of Congress Cataloging-in-Publication Data
Ochiltree, Dianne.
Lull-a-bye, little one / by Dianne Ochiltree ; illustrated by Hideko Takahashi.   p. cm.
Summary: Rhyming text follows the bedtime routine of a baby and its parents.
[1. Bedtime—Fiction. 2. Parent and child—Fiction. 3. Stories in rhyme.]
I. Takahashi, Hideko, ill. II. Title. III. Title: Lullaby, little one.
PZ8.3.O165Lul 2006   [E]—dc22   2005023964

Special Markets ISBN 978-0-399-24787-3 Not for Resale
ISBN 0-399-24305-4
3 5 7 9 10 8 6 4

This Imagination Library edition is published by Penguin Group (USA), a Pearson
company, exclusively for Dolly Parton's Imagination Library, a not-for-profit
program designed to inspire a love of reading and learning, sponsored in part by The Dollywood
Foundation. Penguin's trade editions of this work are available wherever books are sold.

For Edward Bryan—D.O.

To Amy Pfenning—H.T.

Lull-a-bye, lull-a-bye, little one.
Dinner is over.
Bedtime's begun.

Good night to toys.
Good night to play.
Say good night
to a busy day.

Lull-a-bye, lull-a-bye,
put blocks away.

Lull-a-bye, lull-a-bye,
all done. Hurray!

Splash-a-bye, splash-a-bye,
baby sweet.
Time to scrub fingers,
elbows and feet.

Little boat floats.
Big truck sinks.
Soak in the tub
till you're
wrinkly-pink.

Splash-a-bye, splash-a-bye,
bubble-beard cheeks.

Splash-a-bye, splash-a-bye,
rubber duck squeaks!

Rock-a-bye, rock-a-bye,
baby mine.
Sing silly songs.
Clap hands to a rhyme.

Tickle bee buzzes
your tummy and toes.

Peek-a-boo blanket
nuzzles your nose.

Rock-a-bye, rock-a-bye,
my snuggle-bug.

Rock-a-bye, rock-a-bye,
wrapped in a hug.

Hush-a-bye, hush-a-bye,
tiny love.
Moon will watch
from high above.

Hold Teddy tight.
Off goes the light.

Stars will wink,
bright in the night.

Hush-a-bye, hush-a-bye,
soft wind sighs.

Hush-a-bye, hush-a-bye,
close your eyes.

Lull-a-bye, lull-a-bye,
tucked in tight.

Lull-a-bye, lull-a-bye,
sweet dreams . . .

Good night.